S0-BFB-930

Marc Harshman AND Cheryl Ryan

Red Are the Apples

ILLUSTRATED BY

Wade Zahares

Voyager Books • Harcourt, Inc.   *Orlando Austin New York San Diego Toronto London*   Manufactured in China

For Sarah Jayne, the brightest
flower in our garden   —C. R. and M. H.

For my grandfather Emil Henry Schott, who gave me
years of pleasure picking apples in his famous apple
orchard   —W. Z.

The morning is cool
in the fall of the year.
We explore our garden,
to see what is here.

Brown is the soil,
loose and fine,
that's helped the beans
to leaf and vine.

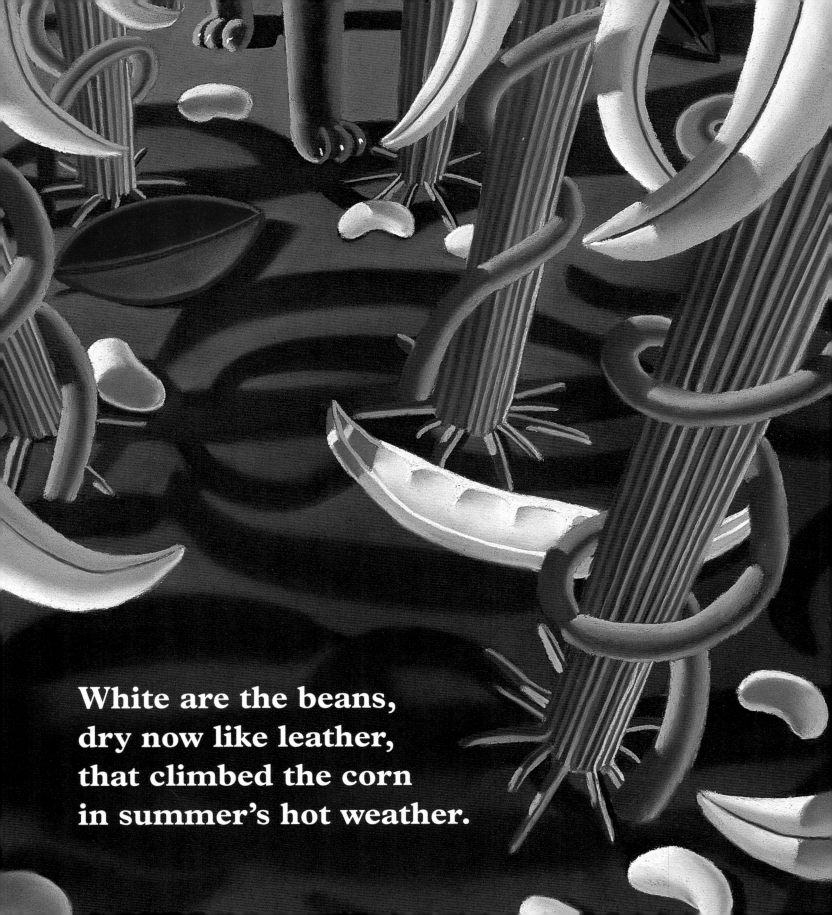

White are the beans,
dry now like leather,
that climbed the corn
in summer's hot weather.

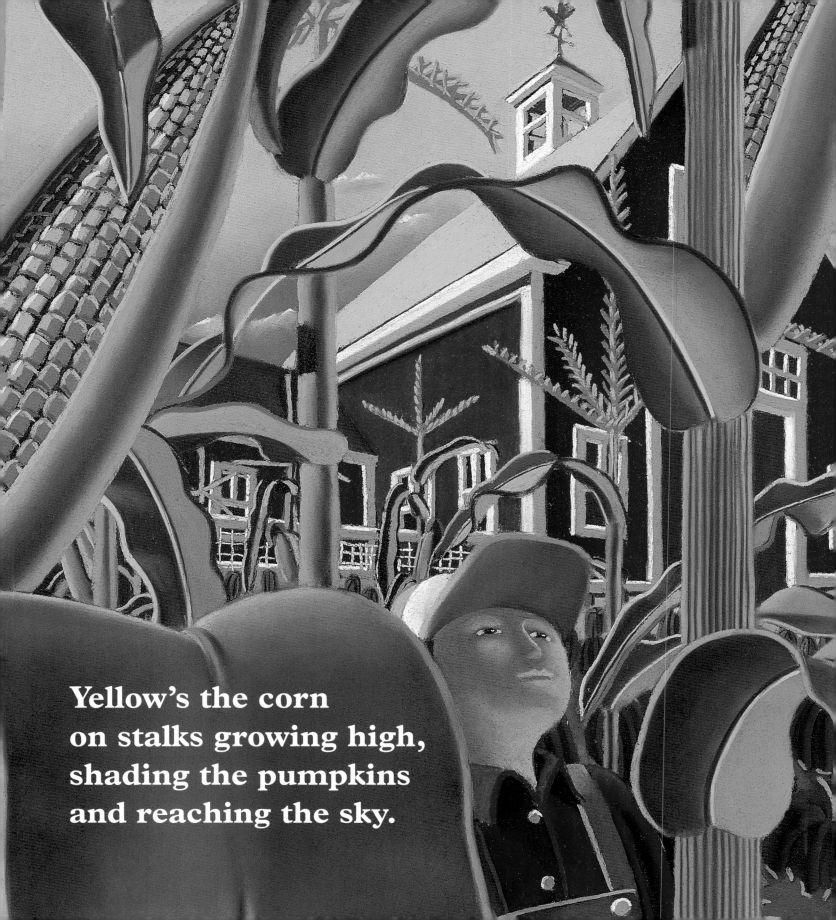

Yellow's the corn
on stalks growing high,
shading the pumpkins
and reaching the sky.

Orange are the pumpkins,
lumpy and fat,
buried amid leaves
like a sleeping cat.

Green are the leaves
that spread left and right,
crowding the beets,
demanding more light.

Crimson are the beets
growing deep down,
beneath the eggplants
in the dark, damp ground.

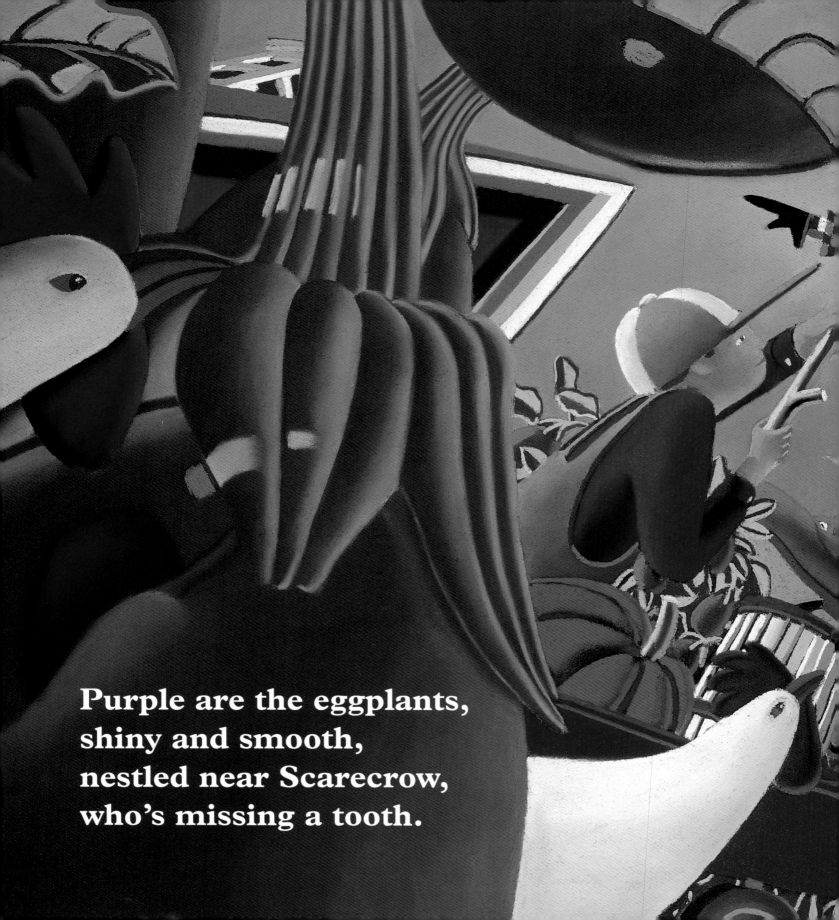

Purple are the eggplants,
shiny and smooth,
nestled near Scarecrow,
who's missing a tooth.

Black is the hat
on Scarecrow's head.
It points to the sky
and the crows overhead.

Blue is the sky
stretched over all.
When the wind blows
the apples will fall.

Red are the apples
felled by the wind.
They'll be cider for sale,
bottled and tinned.

Gold is the cider
that runs from the press.
We fill our glasses,
and taste autumn's best.

Clear are the jars
we use to can.
When we're all done,
in bright rows they'll stand.

And when the harvest is over
in the fall of the year,
we sit and give thanks
for all that is here.

Text copyright © 2001 by Marc Harshman and Cheryl Ryan
Illustrations copyright © 2001 by Wade Zahares

All rights reserved. No part of this publication may be reproduced or
transmitted in any form or by any means, electronic or mechanical,
including photocopy, recording, or any information storage and retrieval
system, without permission in writing from the publisher.

Requests for permission to make copies of any part of the work should be
submitted online at www.harcourt.com/contact or mailed to the following
address: Permissions Department, Harcourt, Inc.,
6277 Sea Harbor Drive, Orlando, Florida 32887-6777.

www.HarcourtBooks.com

First Voyager Books edition 2007

Voyager Books is a trademark of Harcourt, Inc., registered
in the United States of America and/or other jurisdictions.

H G F E D C B A

The Library of Congress has cataloged the hardcover edition as follows:
Harshman, Marc.
Red are the apples/Marc Harshman and Cheryl Ryan;
illustrated by Wade Zahares.
p. cm.
Summary: Leads the reader through a bountiful vegetable garden in
autumn while drawing particular attention to the variety of colors found
within it.
[1. Gardens—Fiction. 2. Autumn—Fiction. 3. Color—Fiction.
4. Stories in rhyme.] I. Ryan, Cheryl. II. Zahares, Wade, ill. III. Title.
PZ8.3.H246Har 2001   [E]—dc21   99-6241
ISBN 978-0-15-201917-4
ISBN 978-0-15-206065-7 pb

The art in this book was made using pastels on paper.
The display type was set in Latienne Medium.
The text type was set in Plantin Bold.
Color separations by Bright Arts Ltd., Hong Kong
Manufactured by South China Printing Company, Ltd., China
Production supervision by Christine Witnik
Designed by Kaelin Chappell and Suzanne Fridley